Elizabeth

Frederick

Garrick

Harold

Kenneth

Lorene

Prescott

Quincy

Richard

Wilma

Xavier

Yancy

Zack

FLANNERY ROW

BY KAREN ACKERMAN

Illustrated by Karen Ann Weinhaus

The Atlantic Monthly Press

BOSTON   NEW YORK

FIRST EDITION

Library of Congress Cataloging-in-Publication Data

Ackerman, Karen, 1951–
 Flannery Row.

 Summary: Commander Ahab Flannery is once again
setting out to sea but not before he says goodbye to
his twenty-six alphabetically arranged children.
 [1. Stories in rhyme. 2. Alphabet] I. Weinhaus,
Karen Ann, ill. II. Title.
PZ8.3.A167Fl   1986   [E]   85-19982
ISBN 0-87113-054-8

DNP

Published simultaneously in Canada

PRINTED IN JAPAN

For Cara, Rachel, and Stephanie,
with special thanks to David

K.A.

To Rick and Sonia

K.W.

If you were to go down to Flannery Row,
where the houses incline to the sea,

you might stop at the gate to the crowded estate
of Commander Ahab Flannery.

His children and missus receive farewell kisses
in a curious fashion, some claim;

for the head of the clan is a family man
with twenty-six heirs to his name!

It took far too long to gather the throng
each time Ahab was called out to sea,

so when saying good-byes now they alphabetize,
arranging themselves A to Z:

First Ahab and Blanche, then Caleb and Derek,

Elizabeth, Frederick, and then on to Garrick,

To **H**arold and **I**rma, and then to **J**ustine,

a handshake for Kenneth, a kiss for Lorene,

A tousle for Michael, a wink to young Ned,

a tender pat placed on small Oliver's head,

To Prescott and Quincy, then Richard and Sue,

then Thomas and Upton, the line nearly through,

To **V**incent and **W**ilma (who kisses him back),

then Xavier, and Yancy, and finally Zack;

With a hug to the missus, off Ahab can go—

not a Flannery missed along Flannery Row!

Ahab

Blanche

Caleb

Derek

Irma

Justine

Michael

Ned

Oliver

Sue

Thomas

Upton

Vincent